**"SEDUCTIVE STORYTELLING SKILL . . .
WE TURN THE PAGES FASTER AND FASTER!"**
—*The New York Times*

Dr. Charles Martel had seen his first wife die slowly, agonizingly of cancer, while he was forced to stand helplessly by. Now he and his second wife, Cathryn, heard the shattering news that his eleven-year-old daughter Michelle was ~~being~~ ... ~~the~~ disease.

This time Charles Martel was going to do something. He was going to find out what was behind this spreading epidemic—no matter how far he had to probe, whom he had to expose, and what horrors he and his wife had to face. . . .

**"CHILLING PLAUSIBILITY AND SUSPENSE . . .
FASCINATING!"**—*John Barkham Reviews*

"BRILLIANT . . . Robin Cook reveals himself as a rare talent!"—*Associated Press*

**"THE CHILLING DARK SIDE OF MEDICAL
CARE** . . . something of a scientific swashbuckler that reads fast and well . . . eminently enjoyable."
—*Jackson Clarion-Ledger*

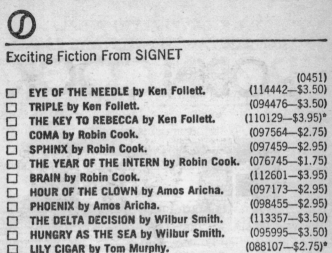

Exciting Fiction From SIGNET

ROBIN COOK

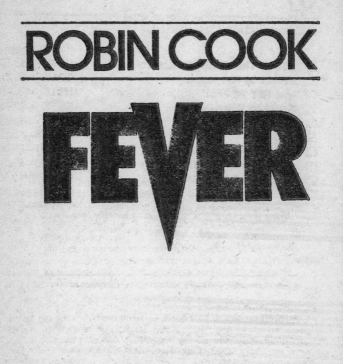

FEVER

A SIGNET BOOK
NEW AMERICAN LIBRARY
TIMES MIRROR

NAL BOOKS ARE AVAILABLE AT QUANTITY DISCOUNTS WHEN USED TO PROMOTE PRODUCTS OR SERVICES. FOR INFORMATION PLEASE WRITE TO PREMIUM MARKETING DIVISION, THE NEW AMERICAN LIBRARY, INC., 1633 BROADWAY, NEW YORK, NEW YORK 10019.

Ⓢ

SIGNET TRADEMARK REG. U.S. PAT. OFF. AND FOREIGN COUNTRIES
REGISTERED TRADEMARK—MARCA REGISTRADA
HECHO EN CHICAGO, U.S.A.

SIGNET, SIGNET CLASSICS, MENTOR, PLUME, MERIDIAN and NAL BOOKS are published by The New American Library, Inc., 1633 Broadway, New York, New York 10019

First Signet Printing, January, 1983

1 2 3 4 5 6 7 8 9

PRINTED IN THE UNITED STATES OF AMERICA

*To the joy of my family—
it began with my parents,
now shared with my wife.*

Prologue

The poisonous molecules of benzene arrived in the bone marrow in a crescendo. The foreign chemical surged with the blood and was carried between the narrow spicules of supporting bone into the farthest reaches of the delicate tissue. It was like a frenzied horde of barbarians descending into Rome. And the result was equally as disastrous. The complicated nature of the marrow, designed to make most of the cellular content of the blood, succumbed to the invaders.

Every cell exposed to the benzene was assaulted. The nature of the chemical was such that it knifed through the cell membranes like steel through butter. Red cells or white, young or mature, it made no difference. Within some lucky cells where only a few molecules of benzene entered, enzymes were able to inactivate the chemical. In most others the destruction of the interior membranes was immediate.

Within minutes the concentration of the benzene had soared to the point that thousands of the poisonous molecules had reached the very heart of the marrow, the primitive, finely structured stem cells. These were the actively dividing units, serving as the source of the circulating blood cells, and their activity bore witness to hundreds of millions of years of evolution. Here, being played out moment by moment, was the incredible mystery of life, an organization more fantastic than the wildest scientific dream. The benzene molecules indiscriminately penetrated these busily reproducing cells, interrupting the orderly replication of the DNA molecules. Most of these cells either halted the life processes in a sudden agonal heave or, having been released from the mysterious central con-

trol, tumbled off in frenzied undirected activity like rabid animals until death intervened.

After the benzene molecules had been washed away by repeated surges of clean blood, the marrow could have recovered except for one stem cell. This cell had been busy for years turning out an impressive progeny of white blood cells whose function, ironically enough, was to help the body fight against foreign invaders. When the benzene penetrated this cell's nucleus, it damaged a very specific part of the DNA but did not kill the cell. It would have been better if the cell had died because the benzene destroyed the fine balance between reproduction and maturation. The cell instantly divided and the resulting daughter cells had the same defect. No longer did they listen to the mysterious central control and mature into normal white blood cells. Instead they responded to an unfettered urge to reproduce their altered selves. Although they appeared to be relatively normal within the marrow, they were different from other young white blood cells. The usual surface stickiness was absent, and they absorbed nutrients at an alarmingly selfish rate. They had become parasites within their own house.

After only twenty divisions there were over one million of these lawless cells. By twenty-seven divisions there were over one billion; they then began to break free from the mass. First a trickle of sick cells entered the circulation, then a steady stream, finally a flood. These cells charged out into the body eager to establish fertile colonies. By forty divisions they numbered over a trillion.

It was the beginning of an aggressive, acute myeloblastic leukemia in the body of a pubescent girl, starting December 28, two days after her twelfth birthday. Her name was Michelle Martel and she had no idea except for a single symptom: she had a fever!

1

A cold January morning tentatively fingered its way over the frigid landscape of Shaftesbury, New Hampshire. Reluctantly the shadows began to pale as the winter sky slowly lightened, revealing a featureless gray cloud cover. It was going to snow and despite the cold, there was a damp sting to the air; a sharp reminder that off to the east lay the Atlantic.

The red brick buildings of old Shaftesbury huddled along the Pawtomack River like a ghost town. The river had been the support, the lifeblood of the town; it sprang from the snow-laden White Mountains in the north and ran to the sea in the southeast. As the river coursed past the town, its smooth flow was interrupted by a crumbling dam and a large waterwheel that no longer turned. Lining the river banks were block after block of empty factories, reminders of a more prosperous age when New England mills were the center of the textile industry. At the extreme southern end of town, at the foot of Main Street, the last brick mill building was occupied by a chemical operation called Recycle, Ltd., a rubber, plastic and vinyl recycling plant. A wisp of acrid, gray smoke rose from a large phallic smokestack and merged with the clouds. Over the whole area hung a foul, choking odor of burnt rubber and plastic. Surrounding the building were enormous piles of discarded rubber tires, like the droppings of a gigantic monster.

South of the town the river ran through rolling, wooded hills, interspersed by snow-covered meadows and bordered by fieldstone fences erected by settlers three hundred years before. Six miles south of the town the river took a lazy curve to the east and formed an idyllic six-acre peninsula of land. In the center was a shallow pond connected to the river by an inlet. Behind the pond rose a hill capped by a white-framed Victorian farmhouse with gabled roofs and gingerbread trim. A long winding driveway bordered with oaks and sugar maples led down to the Interstate 301 heading south toward Massachusetts. Twenty-five yards north of the house was a weatherbeaten barn nestled in a copse of evergreens. Built on piles at the edge of the pond was a miniature copy of the main house; it was a shed turned playhouse.

It was a beautiful New England landscape, like a January calendar scene, except for a slight macabre detail: there were no fish in the pond and no encircling vegetation within six feet.

Inside the picturesque white house, the pale morning light diffused through lace curtains. By degrees the gathering dawn gently nudged Charles Martel from the depths of a satisfying sleep. He rolled over onto his left side, enjoying a contentment he'd been afraid to acknowledge for the past two years. There was a sense of order and security in his life now; Charles had never expected to experience this again after his first wife had been diagnosed to have lymphoma. She had died nine years ago, leaving Charles with three children to raise. Life had become something to endure.

But that was now in the past, and the awful wound had slowly healed. And then to Charles's surprise, even the void had been filled. Two years ago he had remarried, but he still was afraid to admit how much his life had changed for the better. It was safer and easier to concentrate on his work and the day-to-day necessities of family life than to acknowledge his newly regained contentment and thereby admit to the ultimate vulnerability, happiness. But Cathryn, his new wife, made this denial difficult because she was a joyous and giving person. Charles had fallen in love with her the day he met her and had married her five months later. The last two years had only increased his affection for her.

As the darkness receded, Charles could see the placid profile of his sleeping wife. She was on her back with her right arm casually draped on the pillow above her head. She looked much younger than her thirty-two years, a fact which initially had emphasized the thirteen years' differ-

ence in their ages. Charles was forty-five and he ac-
knowledged that he looked it. But Cathryn looked like
twenty-five. Resting on his elbow, Charles stared at her
delicate features. He traced the frame of her provocative
widow's peak, down the length of the soft brown hair to
her shoulder. Her face, lit by the early morning light,
seemed radiant to Charles and his eyes followed the
slightly curved line of her nose, noticing the flare of her
nostrils as she breathed. Watching her he felt a reflex stir-
ring deep within him.

He looked over at the clock; another twenty minutes
before the alarm. Thankfully he lowered himself back into
the warm nest made by the down coverlet and spooned
against his wife, marveling at his sense of well-being. He
even looked forward to his days at the institute. Work
was progressing at an ever-increasing pace. He felt a
twinge of excitement. What if he, Charles Martel, the boy
from Teaneck, New Jersey, made the first real step in un-
raveling the mystery of cancer? Charles knew that it was
becoming increasingly possible, and the irony was that he
was not a formally trained research scientist. He'd been
an internist specializing in allergy when Elizabeth, his first
wife, had become ill. After she died he gave up his lu-
crative practice to become a full-time researcher at the
Weinburger Research Institute. It had been a reaction
against her death, and although some of his colleagues
had told him that a career change was an unhealthy way
to work out such a problem, he had flourished in the new
environment.

Cathryn, sensing her husband was awake, turned over
and found herself in an enveloping hug. Wiping the sleep
from her eyes, she looked at Charles and laughed. He
looked so uncharacteristically impish.

"What's going on in that little mind of yours?" she
asked, smiling.

"I've just been watching you."

"Wonderful! I'm sure I look my best," said Cathryn.

"You look devastating," teased Charles, pushing her
thick hair back from her forehead.

Cathryn, now more awake, realized the urgency of his
arousal. Running her hand down her husband's body, she

encountered an erect penis. "And what is this?" she asked.

"I accept no responsibility," said Charles. "That part of my anatomy has a mind of its own."

"Our Polish Pope says a man should not lust after his wife."

"I haven't been. I've been thinking about work," Charles teased.

As the first snowflakes settled on the gabled roofs, they came together with a depth of passion and tenderness that never failed to overwhelm Charles. Then the alarm went off. The day began.

Michelle could hear Cathryn calling from far away, interrupting her dream; she and her father were crossing a field. Michelle tried to ignore the call but it came again. She felt a hand on her shoulder, and when she turned over, she looked up into Cathryn's smiling face.

"Time to get up," her stepmother said brightly.

Michelle took a deep breath and nodded her head, acknowledging that she was awake. She'd had a bad night, full of disturbing dreams which left her soaked with perspiration. She'd felt hot beneath the covers and cold out of them. Several times during the night she thought about going in to Charles. She would have if her father had been alone.

"My goodness, you look flushed," said Cathryn, as she opened the drapes. She reached down and touched Michelle's forehead. It felt hot.

"I think you have a fever again," said Cathryn sympathetically. "Do you feel sick?"

"No," said Michelle quickly. She didn't want to be sick again. She did not want to stay home from school. She wanted to get up and make the orange juice which had always been her job.

"We'd better take your temperature anyway," said Cathryn, going into the connecting bath. She reappeared, alternately flicking and examining the thermometer. "It will only take a minute, then we'll know for sure." She stuck the thermometer into Michelle's mouth. "Under the tongue. I'll be back after I get the boys up."

The door closed and Michelle pulled the thermometer

something was wrong with the car or something else.

"You," Luck answered simply.

"What have I done?" She drew back in surprise.

"Where did you get this ridiculous notion that I'm not wildly in love with you?" he demanded.

"Well, you're not," Eve stated in defense, then faltered under his piercing gaze. "I believe you when you say you love me, but—"

"That's good of you," he taunted dryly. "If I'm not madly in love with you, maybe you should explain why I want to marry you. I'm sure it has something to do with Toby."

"Why are you asking me?" Eve countered. "You know the reasons as well as I do."

"Perhaps better, since they happen to be mine." Luck stretched an arm along the seat back and appeared to relax. "But I'd like to hear you tell me what they are."

"I can provide some of the things that are missing in your life," she said uneasily, not sure why he wanted her to explain, unless it was to make sure she understood.

"Such as?" he prompted her into elaborating on the answer.

"You need a mother for your son, someone to take care of your house and do the cooking, someone to care about you and be there when you want company...." Eve hesitated.

"You left out bed partner," he reminded her coolly.

"That, too," she conceded.

"I'm glad. For a minute I thought I was hiring a full-time housekeeper instead of acquiring a wife." This time some of his anger crept into his voice.

"I...don't understand," Eve stammered.

"You silly fool. There is only one reason why I'm marrying you. I love you and I don't want to live without you!" Luck snapped.

"But Toby—"

"I haven't done too bad a job raising him alone. If he has managed without a mother this long, then he can make it the rest of the way," he retorted. "Believe me, I'm glad the two of you like each other, but I wouldn't give a damn if he hated you as long as I loved you."

"But I thought—" Eve tried again to voice her impressions, and again Luck interrupted her.

"As for the cooking and cleaning, I could have that done. I know you haven't inquired, but I could afford that if it were what I wanted."

"You admitted you were lonely," she inserted quickly before he could cut her off again. "You said it was lonely at home that night outside the tavern."

"So I did," Luck admitted. "Eve, a man can have a hundred women living in his house and from her mouth. Even in that short a time, the mercury had risen to 99. She had a fever and she knew it. Her legs ached and there was a tenderness in the pit of her stomach. She put the thermometer back into her mouth. From where she lay she could look out the window and see her playhouse that Charles had made out of an ice shed. The roof was covered with new-fallen snow and she shivered at the cold scene. She longed for spring and those lazy days that she spent in that fantasy house. Just she and her father.

When the door opened, Jean Paul, age fifteen, was already awake, propped up in bed with his physics book. Behind his head the small clock radio played a soft rock and roll. He was wearing dark red flannel pajamas with blue piping, a Christmas gift from Cathryn.

"You've got twenty minutes," Cathryn said cheerfully.

"Thanks, Mom," said Jean Paul with a smile.

Cathryn paused, looking down at the boy, and her heart melted. She felt like rushing in and swooping him into her arms. But she resisted the temptation. She'd learned that all the Martels were somewhat chary about direct physical contact, a fact which initially had been a little hard for her to deal with. Cathryn came from Boston's Italian North End where touching and hugging was a constant. Although her father had been Latvian, he'd left when Cathryn was twelve, and Cathryn had grown up without his influence. She felt 100 percent Italian. "See you at breakfast," she said.

Jean Paul knew that Cathryn loved to hear him call her Mom and gladly obliged. It was such a low price to pay for the warmth and attention that she showered on him. Jean Paul had been conditioned by a very busy father and seen himself eclipsed by his older brother, Chuck, and his irresistible baby sister, Michelle. Then came Cathryn, and the excitement of the marriage, followed by Cathryn's legal adoption of Chuck, Jean Paul, and Michelle. Jean Paul would have called her "grandmother" if she wanted. He thought he loved Cathryn as much as his real mother; at least what he could remember of her. He'd been six when she died.

Chuck's eyes blinked open at the first touch of Cathryn's hand but he pretended sleep, keeping his head under his pillow. He knew that if he waited she'd touch him again, only a little more forcibly. And he was right, only this time he felt two hands shake his shoulder before the pillow was lifted. Chuck was eighteen years old and in the middle of his first year at Northeastern University. He wasn't doing that well and he dreaded his upcoming semester finals. It was going to be a disaster. At least for everything but psychology.

"Fifteen minutes," said Cathryn. She touseled his long hair. "Your father wants to get to the lab early."

"Shit," said Chuck under his breath.

"Charles, Jr.!" said Cathryn, pretending to be shocked.

"I'm not getting up." Chuck grabbed the pillow from Cathryn's hands and buried himself.

"Oh, yes you are," said Cathryn, as she yanked the covers back.

Chuck's body, clad only in his undershorts, was exposed to the morning chill. He leaped up, pulling the blankets around him. "I told you never to do that," he snapped.

"And I told you to leave your locker-room language in the locker room," said Cathryn, ignoring the nastiness in Chuck's voice. "Fifteen minutes!"

Cathryn spun on her heel and walked out. Chuck's face flushed in frustration. He watched her go down the hall to Michelle's room. She was wearing an antique silk nightgown that she'd bought at a flea market. It was a deep peach color, not too different from her skin. With very little difficulty, Chuck could imagine Cathryn naked. She wasn't old enough to be his mother.

He reached out, hooked his hand around the edge of his door and slammed it. Just because his father liked to get to his lab before eight, Chuck had to get up at the crack of dawn like some goddamn farmer. The big deal scientist! Chuck rubbed his face and noticed the open book at his bedside. *Crime and Punishment*. He'd spent most of the previous evening reading it. It wasn't for any of his courses, which was probably why he was enjoying it. He should have studied chemistry because he was in danger of flunking. God, what would Charles say if he still be lonely if none of those women is the right one.''

''Please.'' She turned her head away, afraid of being convinced by him. ''I know how much you loved your first wife.''

''Yes, I *loved* Lisa—'' he stressed the verb ''—but it's in the past tense, Eve. I *did* love her, but I love *you* now. It's completely different.''

''I know that,'' she murmured with a little ache.

''Do you?'' Luck sighed behind her, then his hands were turning her into his arms. ''I loved her as a young man loves. I'm not the same person anymore. I've changed. I've grown up. I'm an adult male, Eve, and I want you and love you as only a man can—wildly, deeply and romantically.''

''Luck.'' Eve held her breath, finally beginning to believe it could be true.

''Come here.'' He smiled and began to gather her into his arms. ''I want to prove it to you.''

She could hardly argue when his mouth was covering hers with such hungry force. And she didn't want to anymore.

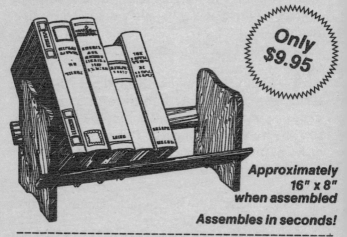

did! There had already been a huge blowup when Chuck had not been able to get into Charles's alma mater, Harvard. Now if he flunked chemistry . . . Chemistry had been Charles's major.

"I don't want to be a goddamn doctor anyway," Chuck snapped, as he stood up and pulled on dirty Levi's. He was proud of the fact that they'd never been washed. In the bathroom he decided not to shave. He thought maybe he'd grow a beard.

Clad in a terrycloth lava-lava, which, unfortunately, emphasized the fifteen pounds he'd gained in the last ten years, Charles lathered his chin. He was trying to sort through the myriad facts associated with his current research project. The immunology of living forms involved a complexity which never failed to amaze and exhilarate him, especially now that he thought he was coming very close to some real answers about cancer. Charles had been excited before and wrong before. He knew that. But now his ideas were based on years of painstaking experimentation and supported by easily reproducible facts.

Charles began to chart the schedule for the day. He wanted to start work with the new HR7 strain of mice which carried hereditary mammary cancer. He hoped to make the animals "allergic" to their own tumors, a goal which Charles felt was coming closer and closer.

Cathryn opened the door and pushed past him. Pulling her gown over her head, she slipped into the shower. The water and steam billowed the shower curtain. After a moment she pulled back the curtain and called to Charles.

"I think I've got to take Michelle to see a real doctor," she said before disappearing back behind the curtain.

Charles paused in his shaving, trying not to be annoyed by her sarcastic reference to a "real" doctor. It was a sensitive issue between them.

"I really thought that marrying a doctor would at least guarantee good medical attention for my family," shouted Cathryn over the din of the shower. "Was I wrong!"

Charles busied himself, examining his half-shaved face, noticing in the process that his eyelids were a little puffy. He was trying to avoid a fight. The fact that the family's "medical problems" spontaneously solved themselves within twenty-four hours was lost on Cathryn. Her newly awakened mother instincts demanded specialists for every sniffle, ache, or bout of diarrhea.

"Michelle still feeling lousy?" asked Charles. It was better to talk about specifics.

"I shouldn't have to tell you. The child's been feeling sick for some time."

With exasperation, Charles reached out and pulled back the edge of the shower curtain. "Cathryn, I'm a cancer researcher, not a pediatrician."

"Oh, excuse me," said Cathryn, lifting her face to the water. "I thought you were a doctor."

"I'm not going to let you bait me into an argument," said Charles testily. "The flu has been going around. Michelle has a touch of it. People feel lousy for a week and then it's over."

Pulling her head from beneath the shower, Cathryn looked directly at Charles. "The point is, she's been feeling lousy for four weeks."

"Four weeks?" he asked. Time had a way of dissolving in the face of his work.

"Four weeks," repeated Cathryn. "I don't think I'm panicking at the first sign of a cold. I think I'd better take Michelle into Pediatric Hospital and see Dr. Wiley. Besides, I can visit the Schonhauser boy."

"All right, I'll take a look at Michelle," agreed Charles, turning back to the sink. Four weeks was a long time to have the flu. Perhaps Cathryn was exaggerating, but he knew better than to question. In fact, it was better to change the subject. "What's wrong with the Schonhauser boy?" The Schonhausers were neighbors who lived about a mile up the river. Henry Schonhauser was a chemist at M.I.T. and one of the few people with whom Charles enjoyed socializing. The Schonhauser boy, Tad, was a year older than Michelle, but because of the way their birthdays fell, they were in the same class.

Cathryn stepped out of the shower, pleased that her tactic to get Charles to look at Michelle had worked so perfectly. "Tad's been in the hospital for three weeks. I hear he's very sick but I haven't spoken with Marge since he went in."

"What's the diagnosis?" Charles poised the razor below his left sideburn.

"Something I've never heard of before. Elastic anemia or something," said Cathryn, toweling herself off.

"Aplastic anemia?" asked Charles with disbelief.

"Something like that."

"My God," said Charles, leaning on the sink. "That's awful."

"What is it?" Cathryn experienced a reflex jolt of panic.

"It's a disease where the bone marrow stops producing blood cells."

"Is it serious?"

"It's always serious and often fatal."

Cathryn's arms hung limply at her sides, her wet hair like an unwrung mop. She could feel a mixture of sympathy and fear. "Is it catching?"

"No," said Charles absently. He was trying to remember what he knew of the affliction. It was not a common illness.

"Michelle and Tad have spent quite a bit of time together," said Cathryn. Her voice was hesitant.

Charles looked at her, realizing that she was pleading for reassurance. "Wait a minute. You're not thinking that Michelle might have aplastic anemia, are you?"

"Could she?"

"No. My God, you're like a med student. You hear of a new disease and five minutes later either you or the kids have it. Aplastic anemia is as rare as hell. It's usually associated with some drug or chemical. It's either a poisoning or an allergic reaction. Although most of the time the actual cause is never found. Anyway, it's not catching; but that poor kid."

"And to think I haven't even called Marge," said Cathryn. She leaned forward and looked at her face in the mirror. She tried to imagine the emotional strain Marge was under and decided she'd better go back to making lists like she did before getting married. There was no excuse for such thoughtlessness.

Charles shaved the left side of his face wondering if aplastic anemia was the kind of disease he should look into. Could it possibly shed some clue on the organization of life? Where was the control which shut the marrow down? That was a cogent question because, after all, it was the control issue which Charles felt was key to understanding cancer.

With the knuckle of his first finger, Charles knocked softly on Michelle's door. Listening, he heard only the sound of the shower coming from the connecting bathroom. Quietly he opened the door. Michelle was lying in bed, facing away from him. Abruptly she turned over and their eyes met. A line of tears which sparkled in the morning light ran down her flushed cheeks. Charles's heart melted.

Sitting on the edge of her eyelet-covered bed, he bent down and kissed her forehead. With his lips he could tell she had a fever. Straightening up, Charles looked at his little girl. He could so easily see Elizabeth, his first wife, in Michelle's face. There was the same thick, black hair, the same high cheekbones and full lips, the same flawless olive skin. From Charles, Michelle had inherited intensely blue eyes, straight white teeth, and unfortunately a somewhat wide nose. Charles believed she was the most beautiful twelve-year-old in the world.

With the back of his hand he wiped the wetness from her cheeks.

"I'm sorry, Daddy," said Michelle through her tears.

"What do you mean, sorry?" asked Charles softly.

"I'm sorry I'm sick again. I don't like to be a bother."

Charles hugged her. She felt fragile in his arms. "You're not a bother. I don't want to even hear you say such a thing. Let me look at you."

Embarrassed by her tears, Michelle kept her face averted as Charles pulled away to examine her. He cradled her chin in the palm of his hand and lifted her face to his. "Tell me how you feel. What is bothering you?"

"I just feel a little weak, that's all. I can go to school. Really I can."

"Sore throat?"

"A little. Not much. Cathryn said I couldn't go to school."

"Anything else? Headache?"

"A little but it's better."